# Murray and the Mudmumblers
## The Christmas Benefit at the Haw River River Ballroom

Written by Bill Pike
Illustrated by Nell Chesley

Chickering
piano player

salamander

Gibby
guitarist

beaver

frog

alligator

Opossum

Murray
lead singer
guitarist

Zeke
bass player

Stick
drummer

Murray and the Mudmumblers, The Christmas Benefit at the Haw River Ballroom
1st Printing

_____

@ Copyright 2014
Written by Bill Pike
Illustrated by Nell Chesley
Richmond, Virginia

Cataloging-in-publication data for this book is available from The Library of Congress.
ISBN: 978-0-9850375-2-9

_____

To order a copy, or for information write:

Dementi Milestone Publishing, Inc.
Manakin-Sabot, VA 23103

www.dementimilestonepublishing.com

_____

Manuscript design by Jayne Hushen

Printed in the US

## Acknowledgements

Thanks to Trinity United Methodist Church, the Contemporary and Outreach Sunday School Classes, Richmond Christians Who Write, the kind folks who purchased our first book, and the fearless readers who previewed an early draft of *Murray and the Mudmumblers*: Lee Davis, Rhonda Riddick, Dave Hogge, Jay Baxa, Susan Forthuber, Hillary Coakley, Heather Lockermann, Joe Vanderford, Penny DeGaetani, and Adrienne Gramberg. A special thanks to my wife, Betsy, our three children Lauren, Andrew, and Elizabeth, our daughter-in-law, Kathryn, son-in-law, Doug, and the relatives, friends, and colleagues who have put up with me all these years.

## Dedication from the Author

To my sister, Lisa, her husband, Eric, and the best guardian angels, our parents. Psalm 91:11: "For he will command his angels concerning you to guard you in all your ways."

## Dedication from the Illustrator

To our granddaughter, Cora Chesley, who was born since the publication of *The Last Pumpkin* and Christopher Schmitt, a young church friend.

## About the Author
## Bill Pike

Born and raised in North Carolina, Bill Pike spent 31 years as an educator in the public schools of Virginia. After retirement from the school system, Bill continued to work on a part-time basis with assorted education projects in Virginia. In January of 2010, he was hired as the Director of Facilities and Administration at Trinity United Methodist Church in Henrico County, Virginia.

## About the Illustrator

## Nell Chesley

Born in Marion, N.C., living in Richmond most of her adult life, Nell is devoted to her family and art. A graduate of Meredith College and VCU's School of the Arts, Nell was an elementary school teacher before becoming an oil painter over thirty years ago.

# Introduction

I have always enjoyed music. When I was growing up, I turned down opportunities from my parents for lessons to learn to play an instrument, and I was a teary eyed participant in the children choirs at church as I didn't enjoy performing in front of an audience.

Growing up in the 60s, I experienced the excitement of Beatlemania, and I also developed an appreciation for the California sound of the Beach Boys. In the fall of 1989, I had the privilege of going out on the road with the Beach Boys as they toured with another American band, Chicago. For six days, I was a Project Teach coordinator, and I traveled with the production crew for the Beach Boys in a customized tour bus. That experience gave me an understanding of all the planning and logistics that go on behind the scenes before the performers take the stage. Tour buses, tractor trailers loaded with equipment are driven through the night heading to the next city where the roadies and production staff unload and set up everything again for another concert.

Without the drivers, roadies, and production staff, there would be no show. All successful companies and organizations have people who work behind the scenes doing the details of the tough work. I hope *Murray and The Mudmumblers* gives the reader a glimpse of how the kindness of people we know and even strangers can help us in challenging circumstances. Our lives can become richer by appreciating the reliable people working in the background to make a difference for us.

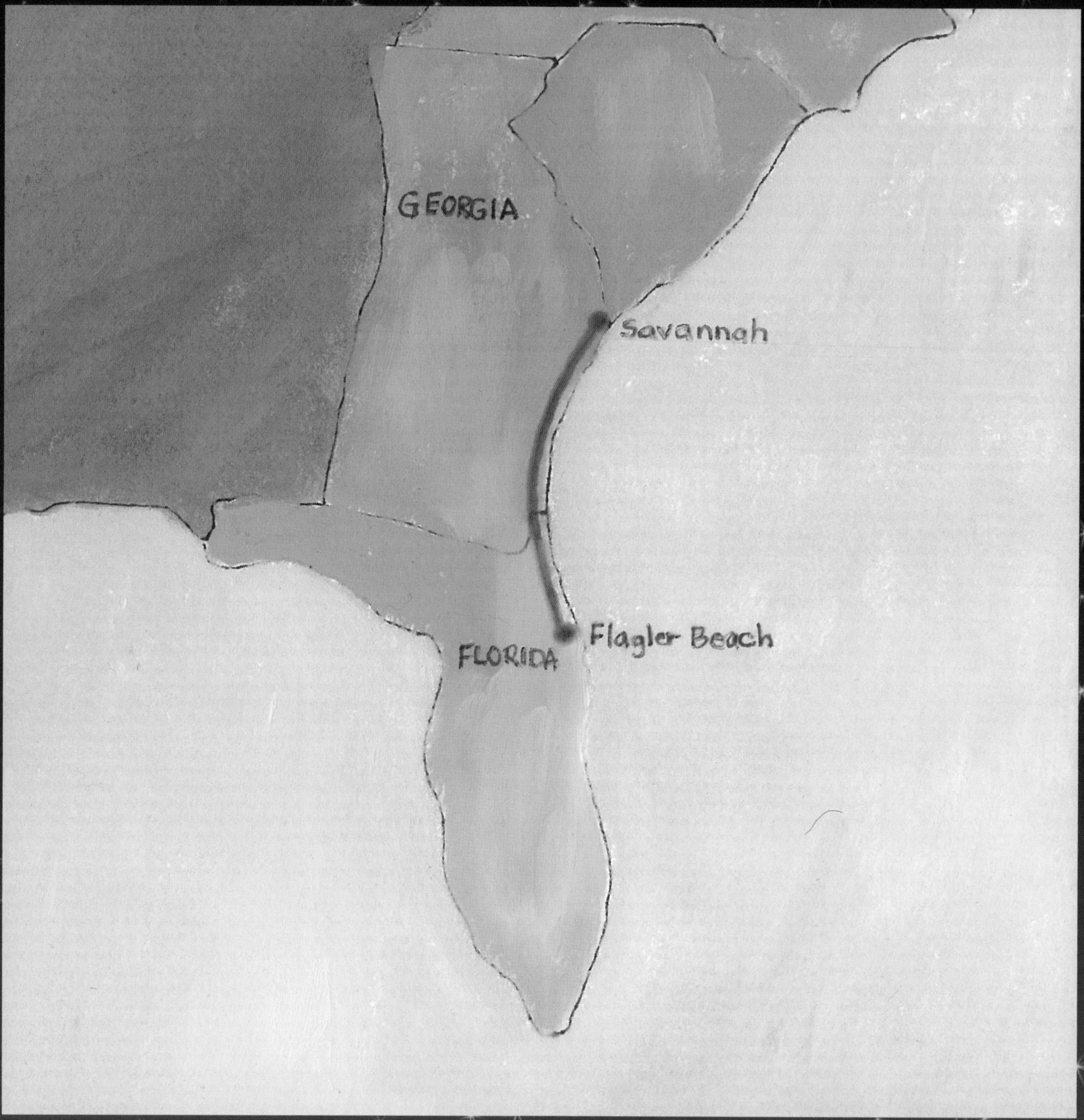
GEORGIA
Savannah
Flagler Beach
FLORIDA

# Chapter One

## Skunks, Kerplunk

Murray and the Mudmumblers slept in their tour bus bunks. It was after midnight. The audience at their last concert in Flagler Beach, Florida had tuckered them out. Three encores, they needed sleep to be ready for their next concert in North Carolina.

MURRAY

CHICKERING

CONROY

GIBBY

ZEKE

STICK

TEX

But suddenly, the sleeping Mudmumblers woke to the screeching sound of bus brakes with rubber tires screaming on the highway.

The Mudmumblers shouted at the bus driver, "Hey, Tex, what are you trying to do, scare us to death?"

Tex chuckled, "No boys, I was trying to save us from being skunked to death!"

The Mudmumblers scampered up the aisle, and looked out the windshield as a mother skunk and five of her kits marched across the road.

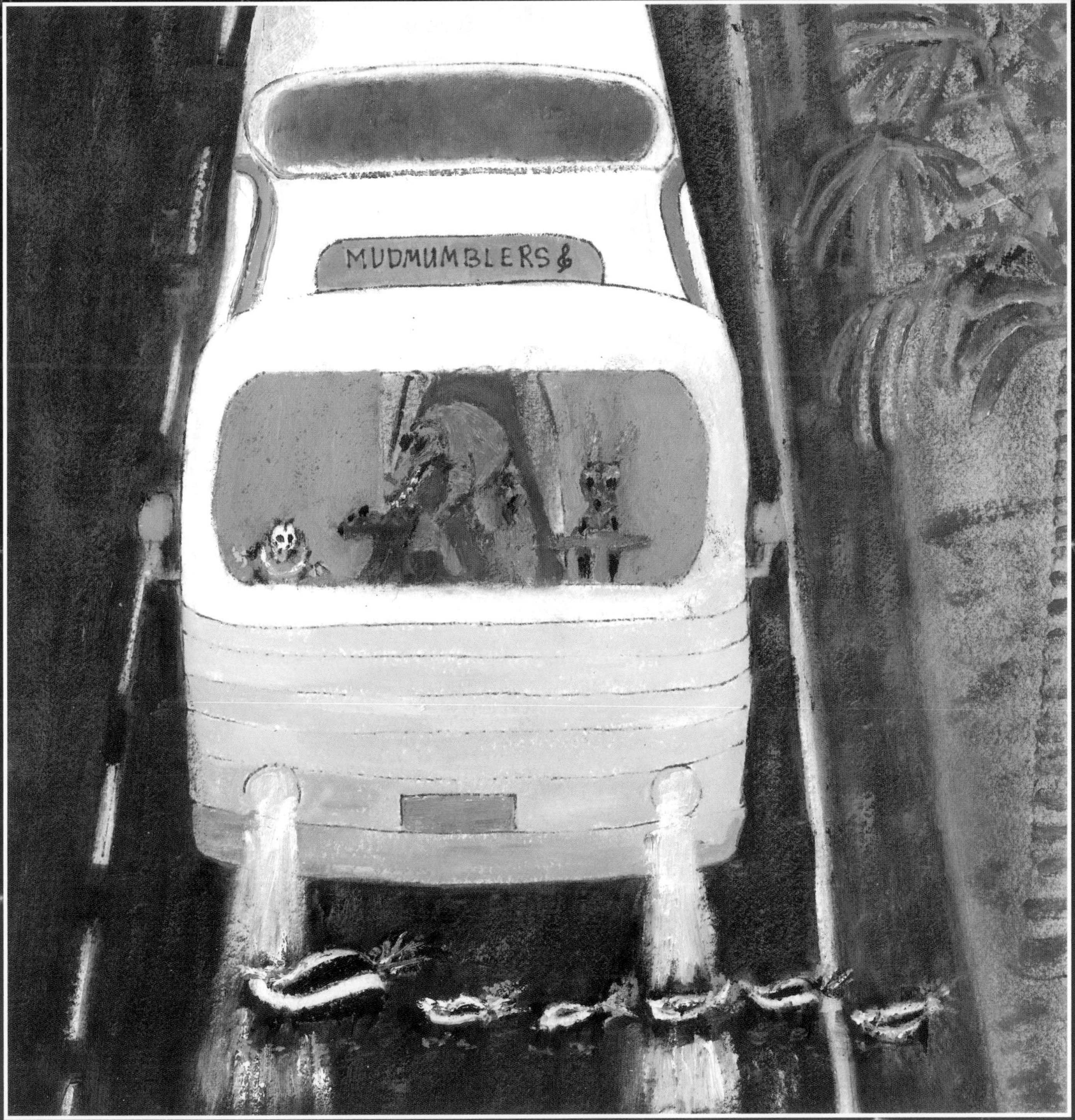
MUDMUMBLERS

"Boy, we were lucky, our bus would have carried that skunk odor for weeks had they sprayed us," said Stick the drummer.

"Good driving, Tex," added Chickering the piano player.

The Mudmumblers walked down the aisle of the bus and crawled back into their bunks.

A couple of hours later, Zeke, the bass player stirred from his sleep. He kept hearing "kerplunk, kerplunk, kerplunk."

Then, Gibby, the guitar player woke from his snoring, and he heard "kerplunk, kerplunk, kerplunk."

Next, Conroy, the road manager for the band, woke from the best dream. Conroy dreamed he had booked Murray and the Mudmumblers to play in the famous Carnegie Hall, but he too heard "kerplunk, kerplunk, kerplunk."

So they poked their heads out of their bunks, and looked down the aisle where they could see Tex.

Right away, they saw Tex had the radio turned up, so Tex wasn't hearing "kerplunk, kerplunk, kerplunk."

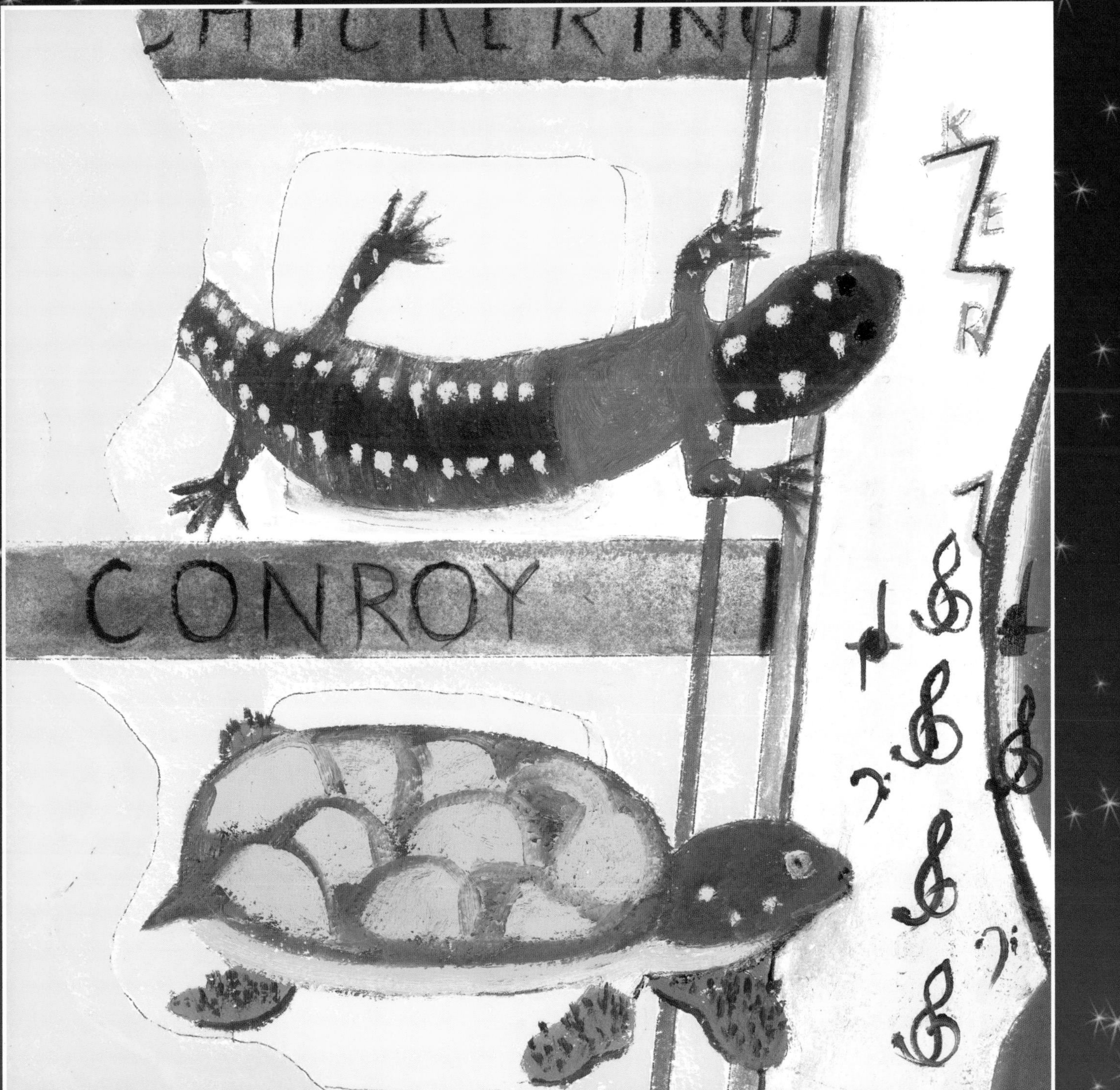
CONROY

Conroy crawled out of his bunk, walked down the aisle, and lightly tapped Tex on the shoulder.

Well, Tex nearly jumped out of his seat. He was listening to the music so intently, he hadn't heard Conroy coming.

Tex turned down the radio, and said to Conroy, "You scared me to death, boss. What are you doing up?"

Conroy said, "Sorry about that Tex, but Zeke, Gibby, and I are hearing 'kerplunk, kerplunk, kerplunk.'"

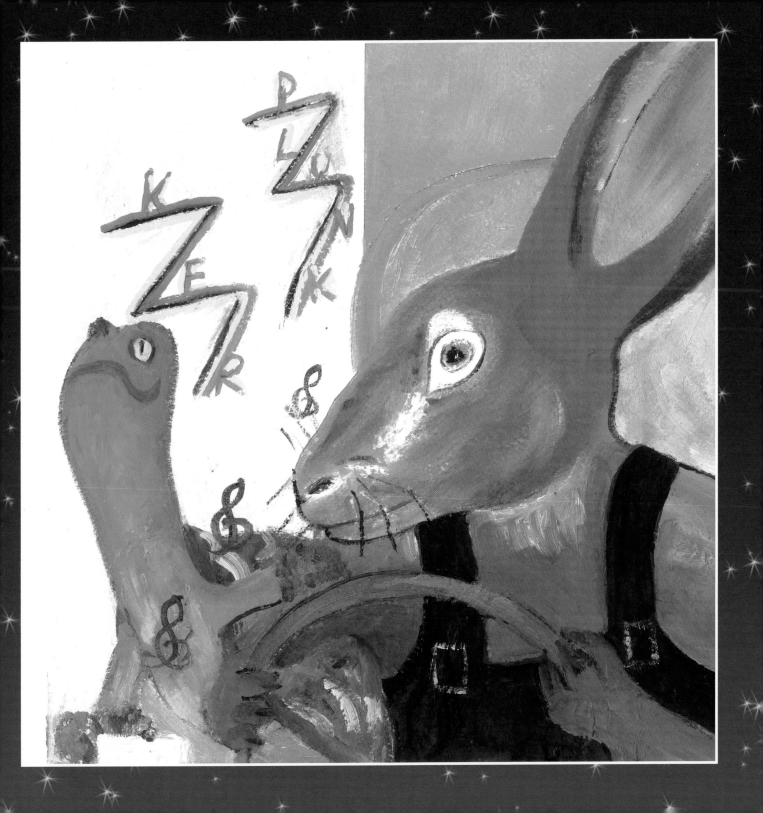

Tex looked at his side mirrors, and he saw smoke coming from the back right tire.

Tex pumped the brakes to slow the bus, turned on the emergency flashers, eased the bus to the side of the road as it rolled into a big mud puddle.

Rolling into the big puddle jolted them all awake, except Murray who somehow was still sleeping.

Tex grabbed the yellow flashlight, orange safety vest, and red fire extinguisher, and went outside to investigate. In a couple of minutes he returned.

"Burr, it's cold out there boys. We're not in Florida any more, that's for sure," shivered Tex.

"It's flat, flat as a pancake, only good thing is when we pulled off the road the tire ran through that big puddle and cooled it off," Tex told them.

"You boys get back in your bunks, you need sleep before the next show, go on back in your bunks, I'll figure this out," Tex ordered.

They followed Tex's orders and went back into their bunks, but Conroy stood there with a worried look on his face.

For almost a year, Conroy had worked on the Mudmumblers' next concert at the Haw River Ballroom. They band would perform a benefit to raise money to help the Sylvan Elementary School install a fitness course. Murray had attended this school when he was younger, and he really wanted to help the school to reach their goal.

Tex had a long day of driving to get the Mudmumblers to the Haw River Ballroom on time. Any delay would make the drive longer. Conroy didn't want to wake up Murray to tell him about the skunks and now the "kerplunk."

Looking at the map, Tex figured they were near Savannah, Georgia. He fired up his old CB radio and lined up a heavy-duty tow truck to lug the bus into the city.

By daybreak, Lucky Louise, the driver of the tow truck, had the bus hooked up to haul into Savannah. Sluggishly, Lucky Louise's truck delivered the bus to a tire center.

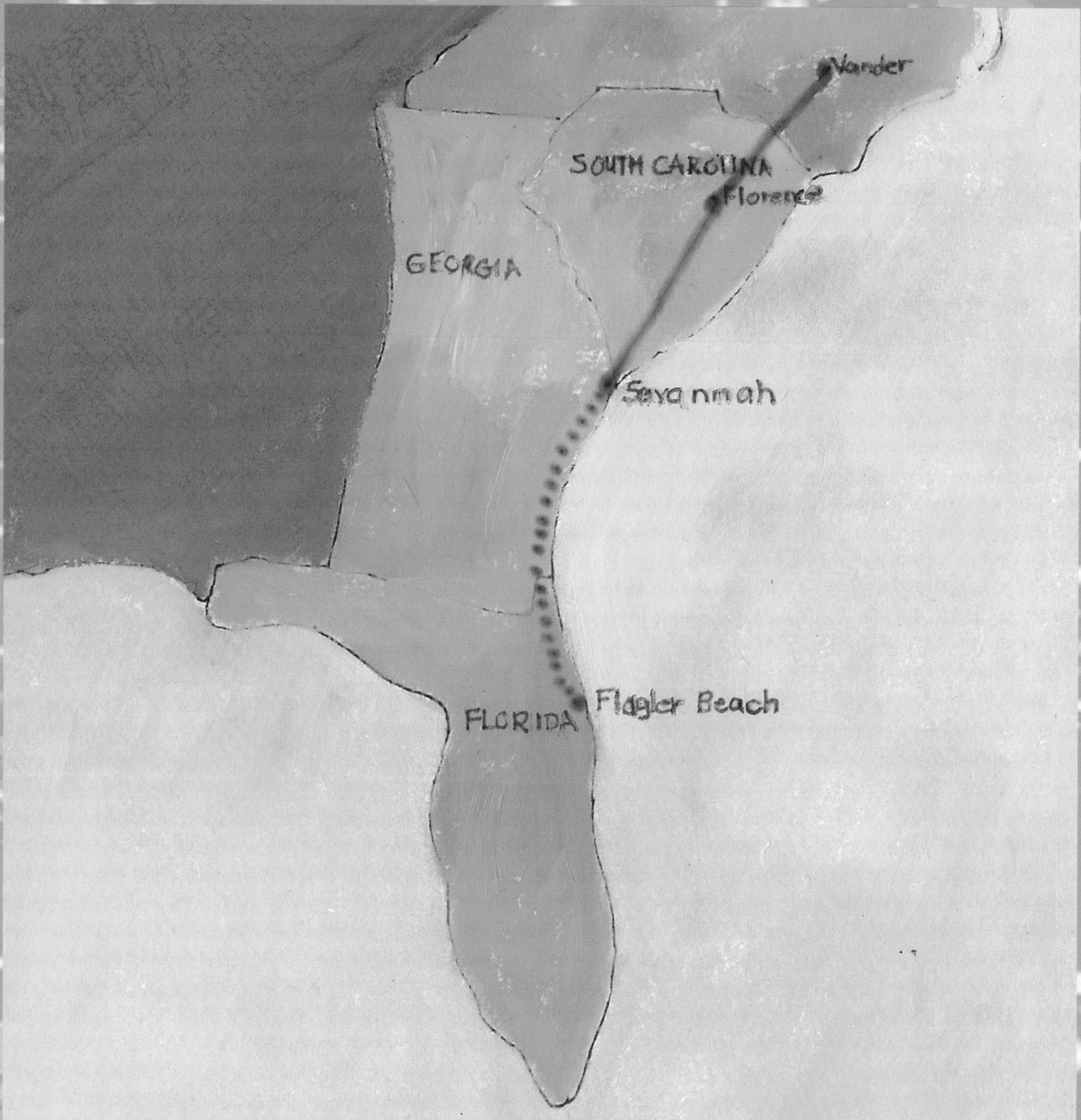
Vander
SOUTH CAROLINA
Florence
GEORGIA
Savanmah
Flagler Beach
FLORIDA

# Chapter 2

## A Change In The Weather

After the tire change, Tex had the old bus chugging north on the highway as they pushed into South Carolina. Tex had been driving in a cold rain and the windshield wipers were slapping away the flattened raindrops.

But Tex grew worried. He thought he saw a snowflake hit the windshield. Near Florence, South Carolina the rain turned to all snow. The trees and the grass along the side of the highway were starting to turn white, but the snow had not started to stick to the road.

Despite his worrying, somehow Conroy had fallen back to sleep, but now Tex figured he'd better wake up Conroy. Tex pushed an alarm button for Conroy's bunk, and in a couple of minutes, a still sleepy Conroy came slowly down the aisle.

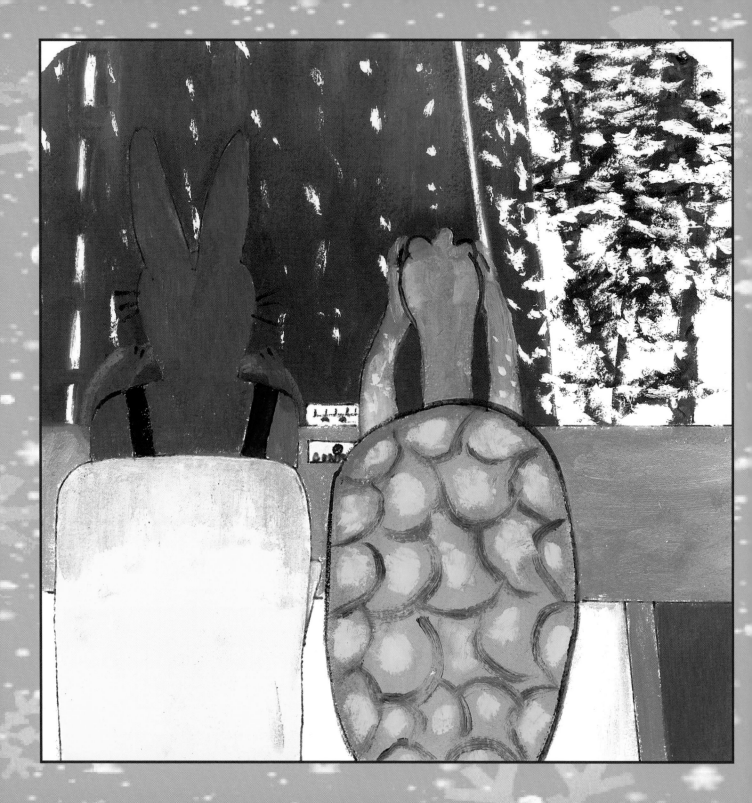

Conroy rubbed the sleep out of his eyes, looked out the windshield of the bus, and asked Tex, "Is that really snow falling?"

Tex rolled his eyes and said, " About an hour ago, a truck carrying turkeys passed me, and the truck was going so fast the feathers blew right off those birds! Wake up Conroy! It's snow! We've already lost time because of the flat tire. You know Murray might just have a major temper tantrum if we're not on time for this special show!"

Conroy's head sunk. He thought to himself: Already more than an hour behind, now it's snowing. We'll need to make a stop for fuel and food for the band. That'll slow us down some more, and we just can't disappoint those kids and their families.

Tex and Conroy talked. Ordering their food to go instead of sitting down to eat in a restaurant would save time.

Tex knew North Carolina was near. Conroy remembered a place called Velma's Healthy Vittles near Vander. Velma's husband, Victor, made and sold biodiesel fuel. They could fill up the band and fill up the bus.

On the road, Conroy always kept good notes related to food and fuel. He checked his old tour notebook and found the number for Velma's. So he

21

called, and the phone rang, and rang, and rang. Conroy was almost ready to hang up when someone answered.

"Hello, this is Conroy Darling, manager of Murray and the Mudmumblers. I need to talk with Velma," stated Conroy.

"Conroy, this is Velma, it's been quite a while since we heard from you, where are you and the Mudmumblers today?"

"Velma, we're about ten minutes away, and because of some skunks, a flat tire, and now this snow storm we are way off schedule in trying to get to a benefit concert tonight. We need fuel for the bus and food for the band; can you help us out?" asked Conroy.

"Conroy, because of this snowstorm, we are ready to close. But it sounds like you need some help, so we'll stay open until you get here." replied Velma.

One little worry wrinkle crinkled off Conroy's forehead as he thanked Velma for her kindness.

As Tex slowed the bus off the highway exit, he noticed snow was covering the streets in Vander. In a couple of blocks, Tex pulled into Velma's and parked the bus next to the pumps where Victor was waiting to fill the tanks with bio-diesel.

VELMA'S HEALTHY VITTLES

BIODIESEL

Walking in the slippery snow, Conroy slowly slogged across the parking lot and entered the restaurant. He gave Velma a big hug of thanks for staying open. She handed him a box that held her famous vegetarian chili, blueberry cornbread, and oatmeal sweet potato cookies. Conroy paid for the food and fuel. He grabbed the box of food and headed back to the bus. Before boarding, he thanked Victor for pumping the fuel.

# Chapter 3

# Wanted: A Snowplow Or Two

The band had food, the bus its fuel, and Conroy had to decide if he should wake up Murray. But then he heard a voice clearing behind him, and he turned around and there was Murray.

"Conroy, how long were you going to wait before you told me about almost hitting the skunks, the flat tire, and now this snowstorm?" asked Murray.

A surprised Conroy stammered, "I thought you were asleep, how do you know about these things?"

"Sleep!" shouted Murray, "I can't sleep, I'm too worried about getting to this show on time, I don't want to disappoint those students and their families."

Before Conroy answered, he felt the bus slowing to a crawl. He looked out the window and saw the snow was really sticking to the road. Tex changed gears to slow down the engine, so that he had better control.

With slippery roads, the bus moved slower, and it would take the band longer to arrive at the Haw River Ballroom. Worry returned to Conroy as he searched his brain for ways to speed up.

Murray looked at Conroy and asked, "You old worry wart, aren't we in North Carolina?"

Conroy thought the bus was in North Carolina, but why was that important to Murray? Then Conroy remembered. Murray's Uncle Tater worked for the highway department. If Murray could find Uncle Tater, maybe a snowplow could be sent.

Almost one o'clock and on a good travel day, they were still hours away from the Haw River Ballroom. With this heavy snow, Tex, Conroy, and Murray knew the bus would be going too slow to make the show on time.

Murray called Uncle Tater. No answer at home, no answer at his office, but he did leave a message on his cell phone. Now Murray and Conroy both worried.

Tex kept the old bus chugging up the highway, but its creeping was as slow as a slug sliding across a patio on a hot summer morning. With sad faces the Mudmumblers stared out the windows at the tumbling snowfall. Tex had never seen them look so down.

But Murray was beyond sad. His heart would break if they didn't make this concert to help those students. Murray watched the snow plaster the land as the bus chugged slower, and then his phone rang.

"Hello." There was a long pause, so again he said, "hello." Next he heard, "Murray?"

"Yes, this is Murray," he responded.

"Murray, this is Tater. I received your call, but your message was cut off." Uncle Tater's voice sounded faint and far away, and then Murray's phone went dead. He dialed Uncle Tater again, but he had no luck.

Murray and Conroy looked at each other. They looked out the window at the snow falling heavily and cars and trucks barely crawling on the highway. Then Murray said, "He'll call back. Uncle Tater always calls back."

So they waited and watched. Tex used his driving skills to keep the old bus from slipping off the slick road. Both the bus and the clock were moving as slow as molasses being poured onto cornbread.

To pass the time, Murray huddled the Mudmumblers together to prepare the song list for tonight's show. Murray wanted to make sure they were ready because the band had to work some Christmas songs into the set. The last song performed was to be special, as the school's chorus would join the band.

They had been working for a while, when Tex shouted out: "Glory be, I think that's a snow plow coming behind us in the passing lane!"

All of the Mudmumblers scrambled to Tex's side of the bus. They slid back the lock, and poked their heads out the window.

Sure enough, a snowplow was coming along with its wide blade clearing the road. The Mudmumblers waved and cheered with excitement: "Yippy yeah, wahoo, yahoo!!"

Tex shouted at the band and Conroy, "You knuckleheads, get your noggins out of that window! Next thing you'll know your voices will sound like a bullfrog with the croup, and you won't be playing the Haw River Ballroom."

They shook the snow off their heads, as a second snowplow pulled in front of the bus. Murray and the band went back to work on the song list, and Tex was cheerfully whistling "Merry Texas Christmas You All."

# Chapter 4

## A Stranger With A Shoestring

The snow was falling heavily, but the snowplows were helping the bus to pick up a little more speed. Tex and Conroy were calculating the miles and checking directions to the Haw River Ballroom. They were looking at their watches when without warning Tex realized the bus was slowing down. He had the accelerator mashed all the way to the floor, but the bus was barely moving. He pulled the bus off on the shoulder of the highway, and turned on the emergency flashers.

A cold blast of snowy air filled the bus when Tex pushed open the door.

Nervously, they waited for Tex to report back. A few minutes later, a snow-covered Tex returned. He didn't have good news. The accelerator cable had snapped. Even with the tools Tex carried on the bus, he still needed a way to link the two pieces of dangling cable back together.

As Tex was shaking his head trying to think of something he could use, a pick-up truck pulled off in front of the bus.

The red-faced driver wore a dark coat and took short slippery steps to the door of the bus. Tex opened it for him.

"Hey, my name is Asa Ambrose Abernathy, but people around here just call me "Handy." I saw your emergency flashers, and I thought I'd stop to see if you need some help."

Tex responded, "Much obliged, but unless you know how to repair a broken accelerator cable, this bus won't be moving."

"Well, I can't recall making that type of repair, but let me take a look," Handy replied. So he and Tex went back out to look at the broken cable.

The Mudmumblers watched Handy shuffle back to his truck where he rummaged around for a minute. Then he went to the bus. Next thing they knew, Tex was hustling through the door and back into the driver's seat. He pushed the accelerator to the floor and the old engine roared.

Tex gave the thumbs- up sign to Handy, who waited to make sure Tex could get the bus back on the highway. Handy waved to the Mudmumblers as they drove off.

"Boys it was amazing, amazing!! I watched him link that cable back together with a shoe string, and then he tied them together with a trucker's hitch knot, and I still can't believe it!" reported Tex excitedly.

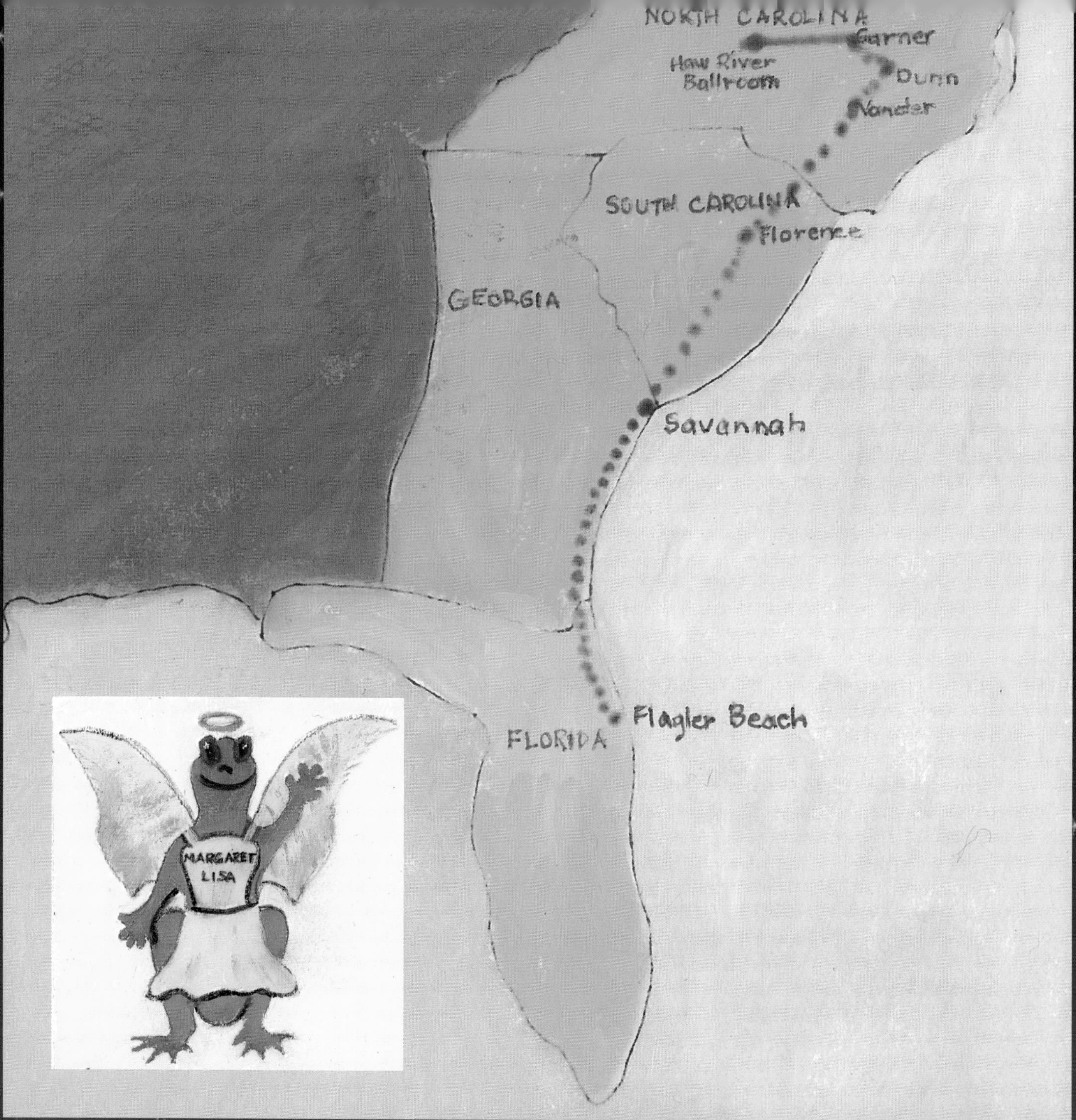
NORTH CAROLINA
Garner
Haw River Ballroom
Dunn
Vander
SOUTH CAROLINA
Florence
GEORGIA
Savannah
Flagler Beach
FLORIDA
MARGARET LISA

# Chapter 5

## A Guardian Angel

The snow had let up, daylight was fading, and Tex was getting them closer to exiting the highway.

Tex spotted the exit for 54 East. Conroy and Murray went over final details, and luckily Uncle Tater's snowplow drivers had cleared the less traveled roads leading to the ballroom.

Following the road signs, soon Tex had the bus parked by the stage entrance. Stagehands helped to unload instruments and equipment, and then Tex collapsed for a nap.

The Mudmumblers were getting ready. Murray was a little nervous about playing before family and old friends, but also he was curious about something. He kept thinking, how did Uncle Tater know we needed help?

Just before they took the stage, Murray asked Tater how he knew the band needed help. Uncle Tater looked at Murray and said, "Your sister Margaret Lisa tracked me down. She's your guardian angel. She always knows your schedule."

When Murray and the Mudmumblers took the stage they looked out upon a packed ballroom. Within the playing of the first songs, the audience came alive as they clapped and sang along with the band.

The excitement in the old ballroom pushed the show right along, and soon it was time for the last song of the evening with the school's chorus.

Before they played it, Murray paused to say a few words.

With a hand over his heart, Murray said, "On behalf of the Mudmumblers, we thank you for coming out on this snowy evening in support of the fitness course at Sylvan Elementary School. I've been thinking about what I wanted to say to you, and I realized we wouldn't be playing this concert without the help we received today from nice people, including my sister who like a guardian angel knew we needed some extra help in getting here."

Murray turned to the chorus, " I wasn't the best student at Sylvan Elementary, but I remember being taught the importance of thanking people

when they help you. I hope you remember to thank people when they support you. Take this to heart too: It's good to help people at Christmas, but truthfully, it's even better to help people throughout the whole year."

For the last song, Murray and the Mudmumblers played "The Beautiful Star of Bethlehem." The sweet harmonies of the children's voices warmed the ballroom and the hearts of the audience as a last flurry of snow swirled in the winter wind.